Laurence Scott

The mooted question and other rhymes

Laurence Scott

The mooted question and other rhymes

ISBN/EAN: 9783337271091

Printed in Europe, USA, Canada, Australia, Japan

Cover: Foto ©Andreas Hilbeck / pixelio.de

More available books at **www.hansebooks.com**

Though earth be cold like winter bare,
Cheerfulness can warm it!

Though life be dull with prosy care,
Yet poetry can charm it!

THE

MOOTED QUESTION,

AND

OTHER RHYMES.

BY

AURENCE W. SCOTT.

ST. LOUIS:
JOHN BURNS, Publisher.
1880.

DEDICATION.

THIS BOOK
TO YOU
I DEDICATE.
LOOK,
REVIEW,
AND MEDITATE.

PREFACE.

The author does not claim to be a poet, but considers his forte to be argumentative prose. However, he has occasionally interviewed "the Muses" as a pastime, while resting from more laborious studies; and having adjudged the "Mooted Question" worthy of preservation — his friends concurring in that opinion, — he thought it not amiss to publish it in connection with some of his shorter pieces, which he does not dignify with the title of "poems," but "rhymes." He is aware that his pieces possess defects, when viewed from the standpoint of a poetical critic; but begs leave to state that this book is not published to challenge critics, but to entertain the masses. All the boon that he craves is that its perusal may render the enjoyment afforded by its production, and if that is realized he will feel doubly repaid.

INTRODUCTION.

Here are many things of many kinds;
Prepared, of course, for many minds.

One may say, " I don't like this,"
   Another, " I don't like that ; "
A woman gave her cow a kiss;
   Another kissed her cat.

Here are some things grave,
   Here are some things funny :
Take which you'll have ;
   You've paid your money.

CONTENTS.

THE MOOTED QUESTION.

A FABLE.

Once upon a time,
The beasts of every clime
And birds of every feather
All convened together,
In a lovely spot by the river side,
A mooted question to decide.

There were all the beasts of prey,
Who made a truce just for a day:
There was the lion, the king of beasts,
Who on his subjects often feasts!
In shaggy locks his mane doth lie,
When his cruel trade he does not plie;
But when he bounds upon his prey,
Ferocious look!   Ah, "well-a-day!"
Then, in the forest his voice to hear,
Does fill the bravest heart with fear!
For when he lifts that voice on high,
Resembling thunder in the sky,
The sound upon the air does pour,
Like waterfall or cannon's roar!
To stand before him, and behold
That eye so brave! that look so bold!
Would terrify the bravest knight
That ever drew the sword in fight!
The tiger, too, with snow-white teeth —
In upper jaw, and jaw beneath —
Sharp teeth, well set in sockets strong,
Stands there amid the motley throng,
With claws as sharp as pruning-hooks!
How wicked, fierce, and mad he looks!
Such bloody looks! such cruel eyes!
Who can behold and not despise?

There is the wolf — old howling Ruin!
And by him stands old growling Bruin.
There are the various kinds of cats,
Down e'en to those which feast on rats —
Wild mountain cats and catamounts!
Domestic kits that frisk and flounce.
The whole *cat*-alogue are there before thee —
All the *cats* in the *cat*-egory!
There, too, the rats and mice
Come freely forth like sportsman's dice!
They gently play with kitten's paws,
Although in reach of Pussy's claws!
Behold, there stands old Reynard Fox,
Looking as meek as patient ox!

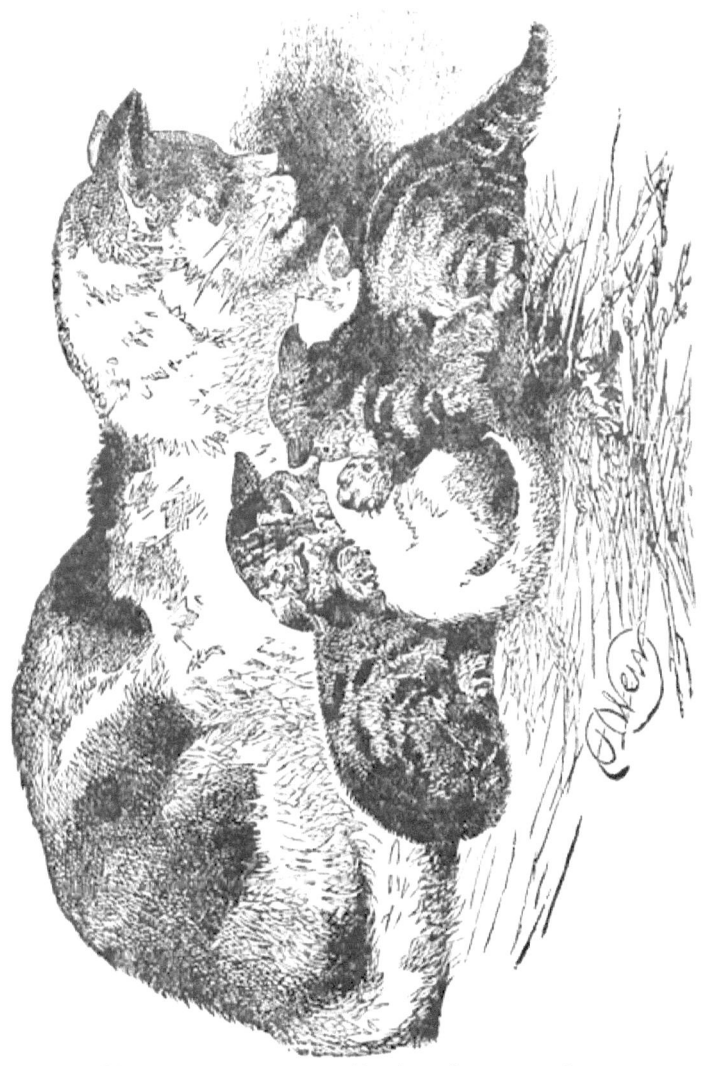

He does not now display his cunning;
He is not now 'fore greyhound running.

There, too, with long, clean-shaven tail,
Opossum sits on end of rail.
The screaming panther next we see,
As gentle now as he can be!
And now we see, on end of plank,
Ichneumen long and weasel lank.
There, too, the dog, who loves the chase,
Comes marching in and takes a place —
All sorts of dogs, of every fur,
From greyhound swift to common cur.

Carnivorous beasts, or beasts of prey,
Were not alone on that great day:

2

There were those of the peaceful kind,
Like pleasant roe and merry hind ;
And, chief among the noble band,
The elephant great, and large, and grand !
Chief in size, I meant to say,
For chief, in truth, the horse does neigh !
See how fine and sleek his look —
With pleasant curve his neck does crook.
Ah ! see what mettle in his eye —
His lofty head — " How's it for high ? "
And when you mount to take a ride,
Your heart expands and swells with pride.
The horse begins to prance and play —
Hark ! I heard his kinsman bray !
This long-eared, stubborn Jack,
To meet the beasts has left the rack.
If e'er Creator felt remorse,
'Twas when he made this burlesque horse.
If e'er he made such work beside,
'Twas when he made his long-eared bride.

Hark! I heard a bell rattle —
Behold, there comes a drove of cattle.
There's Monsieur Boss,
Who looks so cross,
And Madame Cow
Makes her bow.
Next, a flock of sheep
Comes down the steep;
There are ewes and rams,
And frisking lambs!
Next Mr. Goat, with bearded face,
And dignified, takes his place;
And by his side we see a kid,
Whose playful look cannot be hid.

All sorts of squirrels — red, black and gray —
Among the boughs are seen to play.

The common rabbit and the hare,
And mule-eared rabbits, too, are there.
Among them all we see the 'coon,
The ape, the monkey, and baboon ;
Prominent, too, among the gang,
Stands the old orang-outang !

(These animals, you are aware,
Should all be treated with great care,
For Mr. Darwin and some others
Think them fathers — if not brothers !
The monkey, baboon, and the ape,
Possessing something like our shape,
With Darwinites it is a sin
Not to claim them as our kin !)

Then there were present creeping things,
And little insects on their wings —
Among the rest, back-biting fleas,
And many useful honey-bees !
Greater in size, but not in skill,
The " bumble-bee " his place does fill.
The wasp and hornet make some racket,
And with them flies the yellow-jacket.

On those things I forbear to dwell,
And of the fowls proceed to tell.
The eagle on the eye does burst,
And must, of course, be mentioned first;
For not a bird in air or sky
Looks so grand, or soars so high!
The eagle is the emblem of our Columbian home,
As it was the ensign of ancient, mighty Rome.
The eagle high does tower!
Above my descriptive power,
Above all the birds that sing,
And all the fowls upon the wing!

If at all disposed to steal,
I'd plagiarize the poet Neal ;
For that able writer, " I *maun* tell,"
Describes the eagle wondrous well :
" The bird of our banner, the free bird that braves,
When the battle is there, all the wrath of the waves ;
That dips her pinions in the sun's first gush ;
Drinks his meridian blaze, his farewell flush ;
Sits amid stirring stars, and bends her beak,
Like the slipped falcon, when her piercing shriek
Tells that she stoops upon her cleaving wing,
To drink at some new victim's clear, red spring."
She's a mighty bird, any way you'll take her,
But not quite so great as Mr. Neal would make her :
For he says, " She *slumbers* in the night,
Upon the lofty air peak's utmost height ;
Or *sleeps upon the wing*, amid the ray
Of steady, cloudless, everlasting day ! "
But then he contradicts it all,
And says she never sleeps at all ;
But " Sails around the skies, and o'er the rolling deeps,
With still unwearied wing, and eye that *never sleeps*."
But, however that may be,
This glorious bird we see —
This queen of birds of prey,
Is present on this peaceful day.

Whether fast asleep or wide awake,
A high position she does take ;
Perched upon a lofty crag,
With proudest look and boastful brag !
And bends her beak, as if to say,
" I'll only rest a single day —
Let not the fowls fall out and fight,
Or I shall surely show my might !
If blood be shed by bird or beast,
I shall surely grace the feast —
If even one proves a sinner,
I will have a glorious dinner."

But there's no need of any threats,
For not a fowl his talons whets —
No rapine bird shows his claws,
Nor bloody beast shakes his paws:
Though a thousand birds are on the wing,
They merry chirp or sweetly sing!
While all the beasts here before us
Unite with joy to swell the chorus.

So peaceful the owl and hawk to see,
It looks a little like mockery!
While cormorant and cockatoo
Peacefully play with kangaroo!

There are all the birds the boughs among,
As when in Eden's bowers they sung,
Or as they once did all embark,
By God's command, in Noah's ark.

There is the red-bird, with voice so sweet,
There the oriole, with shape so neat;
There is the linnet on a tree,
And by it sits the little pee-wee,
Which builds its house under a cliff,
And daubs it well with mortar stiff.
The ostrich leaves her eggs in sand,
And comes to join the gathering band;
While crane and cuckoo come along,
And with them comes the condor strong.
There is the sparrow, which cannot fall
Without God's notice, though so small.

There is flamingo, very long —
There thrush and lark, with merry song!
It makes the heart throb to think
Of the beauteous, black bobolink,
As he sits perched upon a reed,
And as the breezes bend the weed
His voice sends forth the sweetest notes!
The sound on gentle zephyr floats!
And while his notes he does prolong,
The mocking-bird joins in his song.

And while their sweetest song is heard,
We see the little humming-bird,
Flying among the lovely flowers,
Which cheer the place like summer showers!
Then there's the wren, so very small,
And lady-bird, the least of all.

The strutting peacock next we see,
As proud and vain as he can be.

Turkeys and geese, both wild and tame,
Guineas and chickens also came ;

Many ducks, both tame and wild,
And turtle·doves so gentle, mild.

Then there's the crow with his "caw, caw!"
Buzzard, raven, paroquet, and macaw.

Polly parrot next we see,
And hear her call aloud for tea.
But time would fail of all to tell,
Corncrake, coot, and dotterel,
And every other *avis rara*,
From penguin odd to sweet canary.

We turn our eyes toward the river,
And there we see full many a diver ;
Gayest of all the graceful swan,
As the water she glides on !

With bosom fair and shape so neat,
She brings to mind a sailing fleet.

3

We also see, near the water,
The beaver, bull-frog, and the otter,
And all those of the amphibious kind
Which live by air and water combined.

And in the river are all kinds of fish
That ever swam, or graced a dish;
Even the whale, who took a notion
Just for once to leave the ocean.
The shark and sculpin with him came,
And many more I cannot name.
Perch and trout are here at home,

And all the other fish have come,
Glad to meet each bird and beast
Which oft on little fishes feast,
And know that none have raised the cry,
" Can not attend, — some fish to fry ! "

Let the reader, in imagination,
Behold a great conglomeration

Of all the fowls of the air,
And all the beasts of every lair,
And every fish of river and sea,
Assembled in one company.

They now begin each other to view,
And old acquaintance to renew ;

The scene around they contemplate,
And some of them confabulate, —

They hear a splash in the water!
The parrot asks, " What's the matter ? "
The owl inquires, " Who, who, who ? "
Just as a man comes into view.
He crosses the river, in a skiff,
From opposite side, by a cliff.

He walks among birds, beasts, and flowers,
As Adam walked in Eden's bowers!
But his attire and style of dress
Are something changed, I must confess.
He wears a golden chain and locket;
And a whisky-bottle in his pocket,
To keep off chilly air o' nights,
Preventing ague and snake-bites, —
A little to take for the stomach's sake,
In case he gets the stomach-ache!
The monkey hails him with delight,
And bounds to him with footsteps light!
While ape and baboon both exclaim:
"We welcome you, in Darwin's name!
Sir, we must have a president, —
To fill the place will you consent?"
But he walks on with proud disdain,
Nor seems to hear sweet music's strain, —
For all the birds, of every feather,
Begin at once and sing together,
And while they do their notes prolong
We catch the words of this their song:

"Be kind to all you chance to meet,
Whether tortoise slow or reindeer fleet;

The horse and pony never beat,
Nor trample the glow-worm under your feet.

" Be kind to the wombat and tapir so mild ;
  Be kind to the winsome jackdaw ;
Be kind to the tiger, and don't make him wild,
  Or he'll give you too much of his jaw.

" Be kind to the oyster, ichneumon, and snail;
  Be kind to the brisk kangaroo ;
Be kind to the leopard, don't tread on his tail,
  For he'll spot you at once if you do.

" Be kind to the gasterpod, gurnard, and rat ;
  Be kind to the *natix torquator;*
Be kind to the *rana palustris*, and bat ;
  Be kind to the *tuberculator.*

" Be kind to the bullfinch, the goat, and the scape ;
  Be kind to the lesser pee-wit ;
Be kind to the chaste odoriferous ape,
  To the beaver, the perch, and tom-tit.

" Be kind to the friendly and vigorous flea ;
  Be kind to the bold cockatoo ;

Be kind to the pussy-cat, baa-lamb, and gee ;
  Be kind to the bow-wow and moo.

" Be kind to the phascolome, yarrell, and bok ;
  To the boscowitch, guffin, and skoo ;
Be kind to the screech-owl and bold prairie hawk,
  To the wiffin, the smoke, and the spoo."

When the singing was through
The man was still in plain view ;
For on a high hill he had taken his seat ;
And all the dogs followed and crouched at his feet.

Silence awhile reigned around —
August stillness, deep, profound —

Such as in creative morn,
Ere living thing was made or born ;
Or such silence as in heaven's tower,
When silence ruled for half an hour.

The ass, at length, the silence broke,
And, as in Balaam's days, he spoke :
" I move the noble elephant
Be chosen as our president ! "
But without his host he reckoned,
For failed his motion of a second ;
And then facetious grew the bear,
Saying such weight would mash the chair.
Then the elephant shook his trunk,
And answered with a little spunk :
" I certainly could *fill* the chair,
But Bruin it could better *bear !* "
John Donkey then, some fun to poke,
Said he meant his motion for a joke.
But Elephant had a witty head,
And answering back, he quickly said :
" My ears, like yours, so small forsooth,
I fear I couldn't hear well enough ! "
" Yes," says John, "your ears are so small,
I wonder you can hear at all ! "

"And like yours, so very short!"
Was Elephant's pithy and ready retort.
Then, above laughter loud and great commotion,
Was heard to say, "I make a motion!"
And reaching forth his trunk in haste,
He placed it round the lion's waist,
Then to the surprise of Bruin and Jack,
Seated him snugly on his back!
"I second the motion," the falcon said,
And dropped a laurel wreath on his head!
Then they elected the lion by acclamation,
And with hearty cheers showed approbation!

The lion spoke with pleasant greeting,
And stated the object of the meeting:
"All living things have met to-day,
From Elephant grand to peacock gay,
Upon this pleasant riverside,
A mooted question to decide.
A great dispute has arisen of late,
Among all of us who confabulate,
As to what animal on land, in air, or sea,
Shows the most savage, barbarous cruelty?
I trust we have made due preparation,
For the question involves our reputation.

Speak kindly, but frank, each sentiment,
On justice, right, and truth intent.
If any one does your character portray,
Remember it is the privilege of the day.
I thank you for calling me to the chair,
Adorned, as it is, with ivory fair !
If, in your wisdom, you should decide
The lion his trade most cruelly has plied,
I shall try to bear it patiently,
As this good elephant bears me."

Then a sheep, under pretence
Of relieving the lion of suspense,
Moved that the lion *is* the most cruel,
And threw in the flame a few words of fuel.
The motion was seconded by Reynard Fox,
And feebly enforced by a lowing ox.
But they voted it down with hisses and yells,
In spite of the jingling of all the cow-bells.

Then turning attention toward the old fox,
The sheep espied in his teeth some locks,
Some beautiful locks of very fine wool,
Which from a lamb he did lately pull.
Then he said, " My motion was too hasty —

Had forgotten that the fox is so tasty;
He feeds so well on lambs and geese,
And is ever ready to break the peace!
The lion, indeed, is peaceful as the ox,
When compared with the mean and hateful fox."
Then said the goose, "I second the motion."
This raised a laugh and wild commotion,
For Reynard replied with a great tirade:
"O, you *goose*, no motion was made!"
Then the goose *flew* into a passion,
And foreswore from the fox forever his ration.
She said she thought he was the most cruel,
And henceforth he must live on mutton and gruel!
But the sheep were dejected,
And by bleating objected.
Said they knew the fox was a glutton,
And he must never hereafter have any mutton.
"Your position," said a pig, "is very well taken,
And I hope in the end he will lose his bacon."

The fox was content with the promise of gruel,
For the sake of relief from the epithet "cruel
And thus by his cunning,
And this little funning,
He defeated the intention
Of his foes in convention ;
And before they had time to make their motion,
Had kicked up a dust and raised a commotion.

Now had snapping fice or growling bear
Been honored with a seat in chair,
They would have growled or snapped
Till their power had been sapped,
And with temper up and anger heating,
Would have lost, in the outset, control of the meeting.
But the lion sat calm and made no ado,
Till all of the sparring was about through,
Then said, with the dignity of two presidents,
" Please observe order, ladies and gents ! "

Now the fox had the floor — or rather ground —
And called attention to the hound ;
Said he was the most cruel beast
That ever graced a chase or feast,
"And verily, my tribe to protect,

I make a move to that effect."
Motion seconded by the deer,
But voted down with laugh and sneer.

Followed many a motion and suggestion,
On the grave and mooted question,
Which of all, in air or sea,
Displays the most cruelty?
Fly says, "Sparrow is in that plight,
Because he swallows a fly at a bite."
Sparrow said, "To the hawk it must fall,
Because he eats sparrows, feathers and all!"
And all the chickens in the crowd
Cried "You are right!" with voices loud.
Hawk said, "The eagle is the most cruel thing,
Because home to its young, hawks it will bring."
Trout and perch said to the hawk,
"That, indeed, is sensible talk!"
"But," added the trout, "I'm not a well-wisher
Of that hateful bird they call the king-fisher!"
The subject was taken up right there,
By many of the birds of air,
And many things they had to say
Of eagles bald and eagles grey;
But that their speeches were one-sided,

The ayes and nays soon decided.
Some suggested the shark,
And pictured him in colors dark.
Some said the alligator
Was the most cruel hater;
But many others named the gar
As the most savage brute, by far.
Then they next arraigned the bear,
And argued 'gainst him with some care.
The screaming panther, too,
Very soon came under review.
The condor, then, and many more,
Were the meeting arraigned before.
But none of these would fill the bill,
As most savage, cruel, and ill.   ·
Many bitter things were said
Of rattlesnake and copperhead;
Things fierce, and e'en much madder,
Against the venomous stinging adder!
Some said the hyena was the worst,
And should by the meeting be accursed;
While some endeavored flaws to pick   •
In animals deemed domestic.
Some went so far as to accuse the cat
Of pausing in prayer to catch a rat!

Not only so, but even the dog
Was then arraigned by a hog,
Who caused the convention to hear
By squealing over the loss of an ear!
But among the many that were named,
And by some most loudly blamed,
There was none they could agree upon
And say, "At last we've found the one."

Now, while they were making much ado
The owl awoke and asked, " Who? who?"
But they couldn't answer his query,
Because they were still in a quandary.

Next a ram made a speech,
In which he did the wolf impeach,
And closed it by a motion,
In which he expressed his notion.
It was seconded by three or four,
And spoken on by many more.

They spoke in tones both loud and deep
Of his sad havoc with the sheep,
And many were the weeping dams
That loudly wailed the loss of lambs.
One speaker told of murdered swan,
And many a mangled, bloody fawn,
While with eloquence many others
Described the wretched state of mothers,
Who, with children on their backs,
Had been pursued by wolfish packs,
And all their children and their nieces
Murdered, mangled, torn to pieces!
Speeches were mingled with sobs and tears;
That he'd " go up " the wolf had fears,
And began at once to count the cost.
The vote was taken, and — just lost.

They have by this time considered about all
On whom suspicion would readily fall;
But one, ever since the question was raised,
Has been astonished and amazed
That he was not singled out,
And very savagely talked about.
He is not surprised when the bear
Points to tiger, and says, " There! "

Bruin has hardly made his motion,
When " Old Bruin, that's my notion ! "
"And that's my notion too ! "
Is spoken aloud by not a few.
The tiger now is duly arraigned,
And many voices overstrained
With speeches to condemn him.
'Tis whispered round, " His chance is slim ! "
And he thinks himself, with the rest,
. That 'tis not so very good at best.
Many now philosophize,
And some of them phrenologize :
" His very looks prove him the meanest,
With sharpest teeth and eye the keenest ! "
" If not the most cruel of any race,
Why is it written on his face ? "
" We have his history, not in books,
But in his bloody, cruel looks ! "
And many speeches of that kind
Are wafted away upon the wind.
The eagle now is ready to speak,
Has raised her head and opened her beak ;
But, hark ! hark !
The dogs do bark.

Men too often take position,
Ere viewing well the situation.
That man up there upon the hill,
Viewing the scenes sat stone still;
He thought him seated on a log,
And so it seems thought every dog;
But up he sprang with sad surprise,
Opening wide his large grey eyes!
A huge crocodile at his feet,
Meanwhile had served him as a seat!
The crocodile began to crawl,
The man did run, and jump, and fall!
The monkey hallooed, " Halloo, brother!
Lost your seat ?   Just get another!"
While " Halloo, what a muss!"
Exclaimed the hippopotamus.

When the man was seated again,
And all the dogs at his feet had lain,
Lion whispered in Elephant's ear,—
What he said I didn't hear;
Elephant beckoned to him the hawk,
And had with him a little talk;
Hawk flew away and spoke to Giraffe,
Who was heard to answer, " Yes, by half."

Then for a while he seemed to talk love
To that elegant lady the carrier-dove,
Who sailed around 'mong camels and dromedaries,
And all o' the principal dignitaries,
Including, of course, the eagle and whale,
Seeming to tell them a little tale.
Returning thence on graceful pinion,
Says to Giraffe, " Of same opinion ! "
The hawk had talked meanwhile
With Tiger, Bear, and Crocodile ;
And, of course, to every second,
Some one either winked or beckoned,
For Bruin's motion was withdrawn
By consent of Elk and Swan.

Now Giraffe, with head so high,
Up toward the hill casts his eye ;
With throbbing heart and deep emotion,
Breaks the silence with this motion :
"*Resolved*, Of all the things of life,
Engaged in earth's devouring strife.
Man is the most cruel and unkind,
For war he makes on his own kind."
Every fish of river and ocean
Forthwith said, " Second the motion."

The motion was seconded, too,
By Camel, Leopard, and Cuckoo,
While Walrus, Moose, and Macaw,
Shouted aloud, " Hurrah, hurrah ! "

Then to the tiger they all gave ear,
While he spoke forth without a fear.
He seemed to speak with agitation,
As if impelled by aggravation.

Fiery sparks appeared to fly
From his wicked, fierce, and cruel eye,
As he poured forth vindictive ire,
Freighted with imprecations dire!
He closed his fiery speech at last,
His eloquence being unsurpassed;
But with those who think or reason,
His speech was a little out of season;
But still it had one grand effect —
It made his friends all stand erect!

Then spoke a monster crocodile:
"Though I've been worshipped on the Nile,
By those beings we call people,
Who changing since have reared a steeple,
Though predisposed in their favor,
Their cruel acts I do not savor."

A whaling speech was made by the whale,
While splashing water with his tail!
Do not remember how his speech ran,
But he closed by saying, "I *can't swallow man.*"
Answered the horse with merry neigh:
"You swallowed one in Jonah's day!"
"Yes," he answered with a frown,
"But you know he didn't stay down."

The eagle was listened to with approbation,
While delivering a fine oration.
As o'er the crowd her keen eye glanced,
The vast assembly stood entranced!
Kindled then the imagination,
While she spoke of desolation —
Desolation caused by war, —
Where bloody men God's image mar.
She spoke of thousands mangled, dying!
And of the wounded sobbing, crying!
And how she'd heard the cannon's thunder,
Filled with awe! and deepest wonder,
That man would ever leave the chase
To wage a war on his own race!

When the eagle had closed her beak,
No one seemed disposed to speak.
At length the parrot mounted the fence;
To originality made no pretence,
But spoke a piece without a falter,
Written by Scott, christened Walter:

"The hunting tribes of air and earth
Respect the brethren of their birth.
Nature, who loves the claim of kind,
Less cruel chase to each assigned.

The falcon poised on soaring wing,
Watches the wild duck by the spring;
The slow-hound wakes the fox's lair;
The greyhound presses on the hare;
The eagle pounces on the lamb;
The wolf devours the fleecy dam;
Even Tiger fell, and sullen Bear,
Their likeness and their lineage spare.
Man only mars kind nature's plan,
And turns the fierce pursuit on man;
Plying war's desultory trade,
Incursion, flight, and ambuscade,
Since Nimrod, Cush's mighty son,
At first the bloody game begun."

The president then sprang to his feet,
And asked the goat to take his seat.
The lion delivered a grand oration,
And was listened to with admiration!
His voice through forest did resound,
As if an earthquake shook the ground!
Birds, beasts, and fishes heard with wonder,
As children awed by peals of thunder!
While he impressed with skill and power
What had been said the previous hour;

And in eloquent strains added thereto
Many thoughts which seemed as new:
Told of children slain by mothers,
And of brothers devouring brothers!
Spoke of Napoleons, Cæsars, Hannibals,
And of Afric's bloody cannibals!
Finally, closing his thrilling oration,
Resumed his seat 'mid great ovation.

Now, for awhile all was still;
Parrot was sent to man on hill —
Sent with proper courtesy,
To know if he had aught to say —
Any reply to what had been said.
He merely answered by shaking his head.
" No ! " roared the lion in thunder tones ;
" How often man his kin disowns !
And now I cast it in his teeth,
He readily will fight his kith ;
But to defend or shield his race,
He's very slow to leave his place ! "
The man hearing, heaved a sigh,
But silent was in his reply.

Rejoiced they all, nor longer tarried ;
The vote being taken, the motion carried ;
With the exception of two, they all voted aye,
For the owl was asleep, and the horse said " neigh."

COURTING A STING.

One morning at a leisure hour,
I watched a kit, from flower to flower,
    Chase a bumble-bee.
The kit, so anxious and so eager,
Like cunning fox, or gold-dust digger,
    I was amused to see.

From flower to flower, from place to place,
The kit pursued with nimble pace,
    Not dreaming of the sting !
And did not call a halt to think,
Till insect soared as quick as wink
    High on exultant wing.

I thought, as I beheld this chase,
That kit is like the human race —
    Our race so proud of heart ;
They oft pursue a supposed joy,
To find at last a sting to annoy,
    With nought to ease the smart.

MAN'S MANY WANTS.

" Man wants but little here below,
 Nor wants that little long."

—*Goldsmith.*

Man wants many things below,
 His wants are quite a throng.

Man wants his cigar here below,
 And wants that cigar long.

Man wants his toddy here below,
 And wants that toddy strong.

Man wants his sweetheart here below, —
 He wants some little Miss Long.

Man wants some money here below,
 And will have it right or wrong.

Man wants his debtors here below, —
 He wants to dun them strong.

Man wants his creditors below, —
 He wants them to go 'long !

Man wants a pair of socks below, —
 His washer finds them strong.

Man wants his dinner here below, —
 He wants to hear the gong !

Man wants all his wants supplied below,
 And that he may want long.

Man wants amusement here below,
 And finds it in this song.

A PARODY.

Father G——, that great old sage,
   We ne'er shall see him more;
He used to wear a long white coat,
   Not buttoned up before.

His heart was open all the day, —
   His printing office too, —
He loved the boys that wore the gray,
   And those that wore the blue.

Ever toward the voice of pain
   His heart with pity turned;
His old white hat had not a stain, —
   The midnight oil he burned.

Kind words he ever had for all,
   He knew no base design!
He ran for President in the Fall,
   The second on the line!

He lived in peace with all mankind —
   The Gentile and the Jew —
When in the race was left behind,
   He never changed his view.

5

Unarmed with anything that shoots,
   He travelled the country o'er ;
He wore his pants inside his boots,
   And loved the poet Moore.

But good old Greeley's now at rest,
   His cause he left to Brown ;
His good advice — " Go West ! "—
   With Grant would not go down.

He modest merit sought to find,
   And pay it its deserts ;
He loved all men of liberal mind,
   And highly prized Carl Schurtz !

Those soldiers he did not abuse
   Who dressed themselves in gray ;
To pardon his foes did not refuse,
   But chose the better way.

His wisdom to the public gaze
   He ever brought to view,
And this he did in many ways,
   As he was wont to do.

His worldly goods he never threw
 In trust to fortune's chances,
But lived (as now his daughters do)
 In easy circumstances.

Much disturbed by anxious cares,
 His last race he ran,
And everybody now declares
 " He was an honest man ! "

THE KILKENNY CATS.

I.

Oh, Madame Muse,
Do not refuse
To sing of the cats
That pleased the rats, —
The two cats of Kilkenny,
That thought there were too many,
And feeling their might,
Went into a fight.
Because they were stout,
To fight it out.

At it they went,
On victory bent,
For glory or death,
Or loss of breath.
The possession of claws
Considered a good cause,
And mutual sneezing
A sufficient reason.

Before the fight
They pleased the sight —

Their fur so sleek,
And look so meek;
When the gauntlet dropt
The fiend out-cropt!
Their hair, upraised,
Like a child amazed
On seeing a ghost,
Or white guide-post!
A step and jump,
And they're in a lump!
A scream and a scratch!
A pretty tight match!
Oh, joy to the mouse
That inhabits the house!
A shriek and a cry
And the fur does fly!
A tussle and scramble —
It's no pleasant gambol,
For the teeth come out,
And off goes each snout!
Their heads go to pieces,
For the fight not ceases!
The body and legs
Are smashed like eggs,
And scattered around
No more to be found;

For deep flows the blood,
Resembling a flood
On which the tails floating
Resemble flat-boating;
For everything's flat
In the way of a cat.
The rats come out
And raise a shout!
And all looks nice
To the little mice.
And so always ends
A war between friends.

II.

You may doubt the truth
Of this story, forsooth!
The truth of this story,
So grim and so gory!
It never happened to the cats
Who feast themselves upon the rats.
Too sensible, puss,
For any such muss!
Any old cat
Too wise for that.
By a figure of speech —
A lesson to teach —

It's transferred to them
From the nations of men.
Men go to war
(The thought I abhor)
With musket and rifle
About some mere trifle,
Like kings in the fable
That lies on the table,
Who broke their ligue
For the sake of a pig!
One sent to the other
As he would to a brother,
"A pig that's blue
I ask of you.
Send it this day,
Or else you may " —
Then raged the reader
Like an excited pleader;
For he saw in the letter
The phrase " You had better! "
The fire flashed from his eye
As he exclaimed, " No pig have I ! "
He returned the message by a lad,
" No pig have I, but if I had " —
This not all is that was said,
But all his lordship ever read.

He tore his hair,
And loud did swear!
He rent his coat
And burnt the note.
The look that lit his face the while
Resembled not the maiden's smile!
That war was sought
Was his first thought.
"Ah well," mused he,
" That well suits me!"
Soon upon the field of battle
They drove their men like fattened cattle.
They tapped a patriotic vein,
From which a bloody stream did rain.
Behold dark strife and hatred sore,
'Twixt those the best of friends before.
Fierce does rage the bloody strife,
With cruel wounds and loss of life.
Behold how fast those ranks are thinned
Like leaves before an autumn wind.
Each day, and hour, and breath of time,
Sends numbers to an unknown clime.
The human mind can never measure
The loss of blood and waste of treasure.
After raging long and fierce,
The war each ruler's heart does pierce;

They find themselves in ruin landing,
And wish to have an understanding.
They make good use
Of a flag of truce,
Saying, " Naught can now assist us
But a hasty, prompt, complete armistice ! "
One thus addressed the other :
" Now see here, my royal brother,
Why did you ask of this kingdom of mine
The very rare gift of a bluish swine ?
And why, I pray, did you ever say,
' Send it to-day, or else you may ? '
And why use in your letter
The phrase, " You had better ? "
" My letter said,
When all was read,"
The king at once did say,
" Send blue pig, ' else you may '
Send any kind
That suits your mind,
Whether blue, or gray,
Or brown, or bay ;
And, closing the letter,
I said ' you had better '
Come and help eat it,
As I intended to meet it.

But why did you reply,
' No blue pig have I,'
And simply add,
' But if I had — '? "
The king forthwith responded,
While laughter loud resounded,
" If offence that sentence gave,
To make a king with anger rave,
I surely did not intend it —
I meant, if I had I'd send it."

III.

Oh world of woe,
To slaughter so !
Oh world of fools,
To be such tools !
Such mere playthings
For men called kings.
Oh world without thought,
By tyrants bought !
Oh world unschooled,
By passion ruled !
Oh world of Neros,
To worship heroes !
Oh world without light,
Each other to fight !

Oh world so rash,
To cut and slash,
Hastening death
By wasting breath,
And shortening life
By bloody strife!

Though not yet done,
　I now will close,
Lest fact should run
　My verse to prose.

HALF PHILOSOPHER AND HALF POET.

I am half of a poet —
Ah, well I know it! —
And half philosopher, too —
Unhappy fix! What shall I do?

When I would indite a line
Of poetry — very fine!
Philosophy comes near,
Driving Muse to the rear.

When I invoke the Muse
To shed her heavenly dews!
I soon begin to philosophize —
To inspect with Reason's eyes.

When Fancy plumes her airy wings
And soars on high and sweetly sings,
Then Reason discord sows
And runs the poetry to prose!

Oh! could I leave this world of matter!
Without a noise — without a clatter,
And rise above this scene of woe,
Where Reason couldn't discord sow!

I'm half philosopher and half poet ;
Oh how sad it is to know it.
When I would reason on matter of **fact,**
Then the Muses show their tact.

When logic and skill are required,
My poetic heart 'comes all fired !
When I would reason close and well,
The squalling Muse begins to yell !

To one alone I can't attend —
The other her voice is sure to blend.
But while I study what to say,
I find that both have fled away !

FLOWERS.

[Written upon the occasion of returning to his boarding-house
and finding an elegant bouquet in his parlor, left by some young
lady friends during the author's absence.]

LADIES : —

Thanks for the nice bouquet
Left for me while away, —
   Its presence cheers my room !
May flowers along life's path arise,
(To gladden your soft sunny eyes !)
   Fragrant with rich perfume !
When flowery paths on earth shall end,
May you to Eden's bowers ascend,
   Where flowers forever bloom.

A GENEROUS FOE.

There lived a man upon a river, —
Not a rich man, but a very good liver.
His name, I am told, was Peter Hill.
He had a watch-dog, by the name of Bill.
This dog, of pure Newfoundland breed,
Would often make a stranger bleed.

A merry lad one day came along,
Very defiantly singing a song.
  Newfoundland came forth,
  All furious and wroth !
The boy did shake and quiver,
And, running, fell into the river.
Under he went, — head and ears, —
Enough, I think, to cool his fears.

The dog, who chased him to the brink,
Does not hesitate to think,
But soon is swimming on the wave,
His object now the boy to save ;

6

And together soon they stand
In peace and safety on the land.

Moral.

A generous foe will end the strife
Before it causes loss of life.

CHOCTAW HYMN.

Chehowa holitopa, ma!
    Chesvs ma! a Chesvs!
Hatak yoshuba i kana,
    Chesvs ma! a Chesvs!

Yummohmi pulla pisa cha!
    Chesvs ma! a Chesvs!
Hatak yoshuba i kana,
    Chesvs ma! a Chesvs!

Is si anuk fehinlashke!
    Chesvs ma! a Chesvs!
Hatak yoshuba i kana,
    Chesvs ma! a Chesvs!

THE WORLD'S REDEEMER.

The Hebrew prophets who, of old,
   In rapturous strains did sing,
With countless sages, seers untold,
   Looked forward for their King.

The nations all, with one accord,
   Were yearning for a " coming one,"
When Jesus Christ — the man, the Lord —
   His royal race on earth begun.

And since his word he's sent abroad,
   Freighted with love and peace !
All aloud his name should laud,
   And never more should cease.

THE POET'S SWEETEST THEME.

Had I of all the poets the power,
Just for a day or for an hour,
　To skim their richest cream,
One sweet poem I would indite,
With soul sincere and heart contrite,
　Upon the loftiest theme!

I would not write
Of angels bright,
　Nor earthly things that please us;
But I would choose
The sweetest Muse —
　I fain would write of Jesus!

With bliss and joy,
Without alloy,
　I'd empty the heart's best treasure!
Then sing what I wrote,
In seraphic note,
　And with unceasing pleasure!

THE MARRIAGE SUPPER OF THE LAMB.

By referring to Rev. 19:6-9 and 21:18-21 the reader will be
better prepared to understand the following poem: —

The Lord of life and light,
   The Lamb of God, the Saviour,
In his great power and might
   Designs to show us favor!

He died to give us life;
   A kingdom he did rear;
He calls the church his wife,
   And tells her not to fear.

By his great love displayed!—
   Love equalled never,
Ties of mutual love were made —
   Ties nought can sever!

The bride exposed to danger dire,
   And held in bondage dread,
To rescue her he left his sire,
   And suffered in her stead!

THE BRIDEGROOM.

Behold him as he's seen in heaven,
  Surrounded by candlesticks of gold!
A perfect number, that of seven,
  Most glorious to behold!

His form — how majestic and divine!
  His appearance — Oh, how grand!
His countenance — Oh, how sublime!
  Who can before him stand?

His eyes, the windows of his soul,
  Do with refulgence beam;
Their sweet expression to behold,
  It doth like heaven seem.

Of his heavenly brow and glowing cheek
  The Muses will not sing.
The bee to sip his lips that speak,
  'Twould rob it of its sting.

His voice — nature's melodies to hear!
  All instruments of art,
And heaven's best music, comes not near
  This index of his heart.

But what!   Am I trying to describe the groom
  Of heaven's great marriage feast?
The world itself affords not room:
  The human mind the least.

My hand falls palsied by my side!
  My pen does refuse to write!
The Muses turn me to the bride,
  And bring her to the sight.

THE BRIDE.

The bride to meet the groom,
  Enters the king's highway;
Bright as the sun! fair as the moon!
  And lovely as a morn in May!

She is arrayed in linen white,
  Most beautiful to behold!
Purity of the saints in light,
  That walk the streets of gold.

Her voice is sweet, her look is tender,
  Her form well pleasing to the sight;
Like a city of golden splendor
  Shining in heaven's clear light!

Like a wall with gates of pearl,
  Built of precious stones, —

Jasper, sardius, sapphire, beryl,
   And others, — shining like thrones.

Behold her sweet angelic face!
   Her eyes, those of a dove!
Every movement dignity and grace!
   Every expression modesty and love!

Description to the bride
   Can never justice do;
Possessing grandeur without pride, —
   Patient, kind, obedient, true!

With all the virtues adorned!
   In her all the graces meet;
Not one of Eden's flowers that bloomed
   Was ever half so sweet!

" As the marriage of the Lamb draws on,
   I hear a great and mighty voice "—
Says the loved apostle John —
   Saying, " Let us be glad and rejoice!

" Alleluia! glory to the great I Am!
   The Lord God omnipotent does reign!
Now has come the supper of the Lamb;
   The bride is ready,— the groom the same."

Says the book of Revelation:
  "The Spirit and the bride say, Come!
Let him who hears repeat the invitation;
  Bid all a hearty welcome!"

" Write," a voice to me does say, —
  Says the loved disciple John, —
" Thrice blessed are all they
  Who share this joy with Judah's Lion!"

And after the command to write,
  I see a blood-washed throng,
All arrayed in robes of white,
  Singing a triumphant song.

" To him that loved the sons of men,
  And washed us in his blood!
To him be glorious praise — Amen!
  And to his Father — God!"

Behold the tree of life,
  The river with water clear!
Behold the bride — the Lamb's wife —
  The bridegroom standing near.

Jehovah, upon his throne,
  Utters the great decree, —
Let church triumphant and my Son
  Forever united be!

Then eternal joy and lasting peace
  Reign throughout that happy home!
There perfect bliss can never cease,
  And sorrow can never come!

And now I raise my humble prayer, —
  A prayer to the great " I Am," —
May you and I at last meet there,
  At the marriage supper of the Lamb.

www.ingramcontent.com/pod-product-compliance
Lightning Source LLC
Chambersburg PA
CBHW020035030726
47499CB00007B/2444